THE RETURN OF ZITA THE SPACEGIRL

Ben Hatke

:01
First Second
New York

First Second

New York

Text and illustrations copyright © 2014 by Ben Hatke

Published by First Second
First Second is an imprint of Roaring Brook Press,
a division of Holtzbrinck Publishing Holdings Limited Partnership
175 Fifth Avenue, New York, NY 10010

Cover and interior design by Colleen AF Venable

Cataloging-in-Publication Data is on file at the Library of Congress

Paperback ISBN: 978-1-59643-876-7
Hardcover ISBN: 978-1-62672-058-9

First Second books may be purchased for business or promotional use.
For information on bulk purchases please contact Macmillan Corporate and
Premium Sales Departement at (800) 221-7945 x5442 or by email at
specialmarkets@macmillan.com.

First Edition 2014

Printed in China by Toppan Leefung Printing Ltd., Dongguan City, Guangdong Province
Paperback: 10
Hardcover: 10 9 8

for Anna

There was a place in my hometown where I used to wander
Above the trees I saw a big black cloud of thunder
Summer rain in my face like snowflakes falling from space
It was so beautiful, and then I passed the mountains
I went coast to coast, and from star to star
That's how you learn, just who you are.

—The Sounds

Chapter
One

THE CHARGES ARE AS FOLLOWS-

"SPACEGIRL."

WHAT?

I'M CALLED "ZITA THE SPACEGIRL."

HEH.

HEH HEH!

HEH.

HEH HEH!

HA HA!

HA HA HA HA HA HA HA HA

HA HA HA!

CRAK.!

YOU'RE OUT OF ORDER.

WH–?

AHEM, THE CHARGES:

UNSANCTIONED DESTRUCTION OF A COMET OR ASTEROID NEAR THE PLANET SCRIPTORIUS.

WHAT?!?

IT WAS GOING TO DESTROY THE PLANET!

DID YOU CHECK THE ASTEROID FOR LIFE FORMS!

I DIDN'T—
I DIDN'T THINK—

NEXT CHARGE:

INTERFERENCE WITH THE IMMIGRATION PATTERNS OF AN ENDANGERED SPECIES COMMONLY CALLED STAR HEARTS.

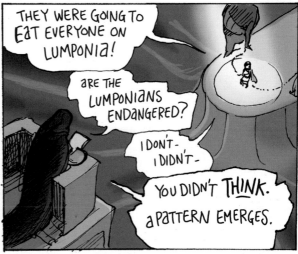

THEY WERE GOING TO EAT EVERYONE ON LUMPONIA!

ARE THE LUMPONIANS ENDANGERED?

I DON'T—
I DIDN'T—

YOU DIDN'T THINK.
A PATTERN EMERGES.

NEXT CHARGE: THEFT OF A SPACECRAFT.

IT WAS AN EMERGENCY.

I WAS GOING TO GIVE IT BACK.

NEXT CHARGE: CONSORTING WITH KNOWN CRIMINALS AND PUBLIC NUISANCES.

CHOK

I GIVE YOU EXHIBIT A: PIZZICATO THE PLUNDERER!

MOUSE!

13

17

24

WE AIN'T NEVER HAD A CELLMATE B'FORE.

YOU'RE A LIVING— A LIVING—

CALL ME RAGPILE.

RAGGY EVOLVED DOWN HERE. HE AIN'T NEVER SEEN THE WORLD OUTSIDE.

SAY! YOU WANNA PLAY EYE-SPY?

26

BUT HE ALWAYS ENDS UP BACK DOWN HERE.

DONCHA, FEMUR?

GET YOUR DIRTY RAGS OFFA ME.

I WAS THE GREATEST ESCAPE ARTIST IN THE SCATTERED WORLDS!

THEN WHY ARE YOU STILL HERE?

GETTIN' OUT OF A CELL IS EASY, KID. BUT GETTING TO THE SURFACE, GETTING OFF WORLD...

THE DUNGEON LORD WILL CATCH YOU EVERY TIME AN' WHEN HE DOES—

YOU'LL END UP LIKE ME.

WELL, I HAVE TO TRY.

YEAH? TELL YOU WHAT THEN, HOT SHOT: I'LL LOAN YOU MY PINKY FINGER!

IT CAN UNLOCK ANYTHING.

GO ON! IT AIN'T LIKE I GOT MUCH USE FOR IT NOW!

C'MON.

CRK!

WHA?

SLIDE!

SLIP!

THANKS. THAT WAS-

HEY!

WAIT UP!

FOOSH

POOM

POOM!

BOOM!

THEY'RE HEADED DOWN TO THE POWER STATION.

WE'LL CUT THEM OFF THERE.

BUT THEY'RE SUPPOSED TO FLOAT IN SPACE. WHAT'S SHE DOING DOWN—

HERE?

SPLSH
SPLSH
SPLSH

CAN'T YOU TELL?

THEY'RE USING HER FOR POWER.

NOW HURRY! THOSE GUARDS WILL BE HERE ANY SECOND.

ZITA!

THIS IS WRONG.

YOU CAN'T SAVE IT!

THERE'S NO TIME!

HNH!

FOSH!

THERE THEY ARE.

ZOK!

WAIT FOR ME!

GOT HER.

WHAT ABOUT THE GHOST?

TIME FOR HIM LATER.

THE MASTER WANTS THIS ONE.

AH.

ZITA.

THE CRIME GIRL.

YOU KNOW, MY GUARDS TOOK a SAMPLE OF YOUR BLOOD WHEN YOU WERE PROCESSED.

I USED IT TO TRACE YOUR PLANET OF ORIGIN.

...

AHH.

SUCH a PRETTY WORLD.

SUCH an UNSUSPECTING WORLD...

CLICK

MONSTER!

SHE'S LOOSE!

Chapter
Three

SMEK

THE GIRL!

LADIES AND GENTLEMEN AND VARIATIONS THEREUPON! WELCOME TO OUR MAIN EVENT!

LET'S MAKE SOME NOISE FOR OUR REIGNING CHAMPION-

COMMANDANT CHOMPERS!

CHOMP CHOMP!

AND OUR (HEH HEH) CHALLENGER, A SCRAPPY OLD H.A.M.B.O. UNIT CALLED-

ONE!

EH?

HUFF
HUFF!

LISTEN, BOYS—

SKWAKER AND I WERE HAVING A PRIVATE CHAT.

LA!

CLANG!

FLING!

FUP!

TIME TO WORK! MOVE IT ALONG!

SQUEE SQUEE!

THWAK!

CRACK!

WHEEZE!

BRAAT!

BRAAT!

BRAAT

DING.

HEEEY KID! HOW WAS WORK?

KID?

FLOMP.

SO YOU GONNA TRY ANOTHER ESCAPE? IF YOU THOUGHT MY FINGER WAS FANCY YOU SHOULD SEE WHAT MY TOES CAN DO!

SO HOW 'BOUT IT? YOU GONNA TRY AGAIN? KID?

NO.

YOU.

YOU HAVE AN ALTERNATE WORK DESIGNATION TODAY.

CHINK CHINK

WHAK! THWAK!

CRAK

SMACK!

YOU WILL BEGIN HERE.

82

BEGIN.

DO IT.
OR YOUR RODENT PAYS THE PRICE.

CRACK!

TRY TO KEEP UP THIS TIME.

ZITA?

WE COULD HAVE SAVED HIM.

YOU CAN'T SAVE EVERYBODY, ZITA.

HOW DO YOU KNOW? YOU DON'T KNOW ANYTHING ABOUT ME!

YOU MIGHT BE SURPRISED.

YEAH? SURPRISE ME!

WHAT DO WE DO NOW?

SSSSSSS!

NOW WE GO OFF GRID.

Chapter
Four

RATTLES? WE NEED A PICKUP.

COUGH!

CAN YOU LOCK ON TO THE -COUGH COUGH!- COMMUNICATOR?

RATTLE CLICK.

I KNOW IT'LL TAKE TIME, JUST- COUGH COUGH!

JUST DO THE BEST YOU CAN.

CLANK

MAYBE WE CAN WAIT DOWN HERE!

WHAT IS THIS PLACE?

SOME KIND OF WAREHOUSE.

THIS MUST BE WHERE THEY PUT EVERYTHING THEY TAKE FROM THE PRISONERS.

WE SHOULD LOOK AROUND FOR SOMETHING USEFUL.

HOLD ON!

YOU STILL HAVEN'T TOLD ME WHAT YOU'RE EVEN **DOING HERE!**

YOU DON'T REMEMBER?

YOU PUSHED THAT **STUPID RED BUTTON** EVEN THOUGH I TOLD YOU **NOT TO!**

BUT I SAVED YOU.

DID YOU?

CH·CHAK

RUN.

WH-WHAT?

BRAKKA BRAKKA!

RUN!

FOOM!

THUMP THUMP

WH-WHAT SHOULD WE-

SPLIT UP.

WHAT?!?

I HAVE AN IDEA.

YOU WERE RIGHT, JOSEPH.

WE NEED TO SEARCH FOR SOMETHING USEFUL.

THUMP THUMP

I'LL HOLD IT OFF— GIVE YOU A HEAD START.

LET'S SEE WHAT THIS DOES.

FOOSH!

OKAY-

CLAMP!

RAA!

FLING!

oOF!

... ONE?

RATTLE RATTLE CLICK.

THAT'S FOUR.

HE'S ON OUR SIDE.

JOSEPH!

OH, AND I FOUND A LITTLE FORCEFIELD GENERATOR.

BUT I DIDN'T.

THE CONNECTION BROKE AND HUNDREDS OF PORTALS OPENED.

I ENDED UP ON A PRETTY BAD WORLD.

I DIDN'T MAKE FRIENDS OR BECOME A HERO LIKE YOU. I WAS PICKED UP BY SLAVERS.

CHOBBLE CHOBBLE!

BUT I LEARNED TO SURVIVE. I GOT PRETTY GOOD AT SMALL ROBOTICS REPAIR AND WAS SOLD SHIP TO SHIP.

UNTIL THE LAST SHIP I WORKED ON WAS STOPPED BY THE DOOM SQUAD.

TURNS OUT SLAVES DON'T GET ESCAPE PODS.

I ENDED UP IN ONE OF THE DEEP CELLS, AND THAT'S WHERE I FOUND FOUR.

OR WHAT WAS LEFT OF HIM.

AND THEN WHAT? HOW DID YOU GET—

YAWN!

JOSEPH?

Z

Chapter
Five

119

CLOK.

YAWN!

WHAT'S THIS?

SECURITY FEED.

CLIK

I TRY TO KEEP AN EYE ON THE DUNGEONS.

flip

HARD TO SEE.

IT'S NOT ALWAYS THIS GRAINY.

THERE'S SOME KIND OF WEIRD INTERFERENCE.

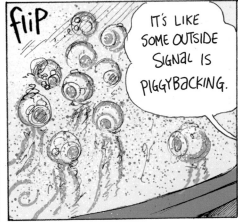

flip

IT'S LIKE SOME OUTSIDE SIGNAL IS PIGGYBACKING.

BUT IT'S NOT IMPORTANT! ZITA, NOW THAT YOU'RE HERE WE MAY ACTUALLY HAVE A CHANCE OF GETTING-

STOP!

PIZZICATO.

121

HE'S ALIVE.

ZITA, YOU CAN'T-

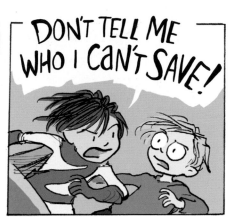

DON'T TELL ME WHO I CAN'T SAVE!

THE DUNGEON LORD HAS AN ARMY, ZITA!

THAT'S WHY WE HAVE TO STOP HIM.

YOU KNOW WHAT HE PLANS TO DO IF HE FINDS THE CRYSTAL.

I KNOW HE'S GOING AFTER SOME PLANET, BUT WE'RE JUST KIDS, ZITA! IT'S NOT OUR JOB TO-

IT'S EARTH, JOSEPH.

WH- WHAT?

122

IT MUST HAVE SLIPPED ITSELF INTO MY POCKET.

I THINK IT CHOSE ME.

DO YOU KNOW WHAT THIS MEANS?

WE CAN GO HOME! WE CAN GO RIGHT NOW AND THE DUNGEON LORD WON'T BE ABLE TO FOLLOW!

WAS IT BECAUSE I TRIED TO HELP THAT OTHER PRISONER?

OR-

BECAUSE I WAS TRYING TO SAVE-

NO.

WHAT?

PIPER!

MADRIGAL!

WE'RE WORKING TOGETHER.

TEMPORARILY.

Strong Strong Star help find lost girl!

YOUR LARGENESS IS BLOCKING THE MONITOR!

WE WILL LAY WASTE TO THIS FOUL WORLD TO RESCUE YOU.

128

FIRE WILL RAIN DOWN FROM THE SKY AS WE-

WHAT IS HE DOING THERE?!?

ZITA! TEAR OUT HIS CIRCUITS BEFORE HE RECHARGES!

MOVE BACK, ONE.

LISTEN, ZITA, MADRIGAL AND I HAVE CLOAKED THE SHIP FOR SNEAKING DOWN TO THE SURFACE -

BUT THOSE DUNGEONS ARE LOCKED TIGHT.

LEAVE THAT TO ME, WE'VE GOT THE ONE THING THE DUNGEON LORD WANTS.

WE'LL USE IT AS BAIT!

NO! THAT AIN'T RIGHT NEITHER!

SORRY, FEMUR.

"SORRY" AIN'T GONNA PUT MY HEAD ON STRAIGHT!

PLINK

HEEEEY! IT'S YOUR PINKY BONE!

NEVER MIND THAT, RAGGY, LOOK!

FOOSH!

OOOH.

QUIET, YOU!

YOU GOT OFF EASY.

SAY, WHAT'S THAT UP AHEAD, BOSS?

EH?

WELL, IF IT ISN'T THE "GHOST" OF DUNGEON WORLD.

IT'S ABOUT TIME YOU AND I—

I'M COMING!

Eh?

DON'T START WITHOUT ME!

THOSE —HUFF— THOSE ARE SOME LONG HALLWAYS!

"CORRIDORS."

WHAT?

THEY'RE "CORRIDORS."

OH. WELL THOSE ARE SOME LONG—

HEY!

AND THE BONES MAKE A SORT OF CRUNCHING SOUND...

CREAK!

AH.

THE CRYSTAL.

GIVE IT TO ME.

I WILL NOT BARGAIN.

GIVE IT TO ME!

IF YOU WANT TO KNOW WHERE THE CRYSTAL IS, YOU'LL DO WHAT WE SAY.

YOU CAN START BY FREEING PIZZICATO.

LOW BAT!

VERY WELL. WE'LL PLAY YOUR GAME FOR NOW.

BUT YOU KNOW THIS WON'T END WELL FOR YOU.

OH, THESE SILLY LOCKS.

HE'S STALLING, ZITA.

HE KNOWS THAT A TWO-PERSON FORCEFIELD IS STRAINING THE BATTERY.

WE CAN DO THIS, JOSEPH.

DON'T BE A COWARD.

SHOVE

WELL WELL WELL...

I HAVE THE CRYSTAL RIGHT HERE.

YOU DO EXACTLY AS I SAY!

OH, OF COURSE!

DON'T BE STUPID, JOSEPH! YOU CAN'T TRUST HIM! HE'S GOING TO-

MPH MMFF!

AND WHAT ARE YOUR DEMANDS?

WELL.

HERE WE ARE.

sniff!

YOU'LL HAVE TO SHUT DOWN THAT FORCEFIELD TO GIVE ME THE DEVICE.

I-I...

DON'T TELL ME YOU'VE DEVELOPED A SUDDEN LACK OF TRUST?

So... WHY WE GOTTA GUARD DIS RAT AGAIN?

BECAUSE YOU ARE HIRED THUGS.

IT IS YOUR LOT.

SEE, YOU SAY "HIRED" BUT I DON'T REMEMBER GETTIN' PAID.

YOUR PEOPLE HAVE BEEN PROMISED ONE OF EARTH'S CONTINENTS.

?

GRR.

OKAY, FISTICUFFS.

CLONK

YOU KNOW I HAD THAT UNDER CONTROL, RIGHT?

YOU'RE NO FIGHTER.

CHIRRIP!

MOUSE!

HE'S UNDER SOME KIND OF SEDATIVE.

I'M SHUTTING IT DOWN. YOU JUST PICK THE LOCK.

GOT IT.

CHANK

THERE WE GO, OLD FRIEND.

YOU'LL BE GOOD AS NEW IN A FEW MOMENTS.

MROW!

GLISSANDO!

YOU FOUND US, CLEVER BOY.

PRRR... PRRRR.....

HE'S... SMALLER THAN I REMEMBER.

snif

BUT THAT WILL WEAR OFF SOON ENOUGH.

BOOM!

THERE IS SOME KIND OF DISTURBANCE ON THE EXECUTION LEVEL.

I HAVE CREATED A SHORTCUT!

THEN WHAT ARE WE WAITING FOR?

LET'S FIND ZITA!

WH-WHAT ARE WE DOING?

P. PIPER SAID TO S-S-STAY WITH THE SHIP.

Strong Strong look outside.

DOP!

B-BUT I'M NO GOOD AT SNEAKING!

IT GIVES ME THE SQUEAKS.

shh...

YOU'RE NOT THINKING OF BACKING OUT OF OUR AGREEMENT?

HOW - HOW DO I KNOW YOU'LL KEEP YOUR PROMISE?

SHALL I TELL YOU WHAT I KNOW?

I KNOW THE BATTERY ON THAT FORCEFIELD WILL LAST ONLY A FEW MOMENTS MORE...

FZZT!

YOU HAVE NO CHOICE BUT TO TRUST ME.

RATTLE
CLICK

HE SAYS HE WANTS TO FIND JOSEPH—

SAY THE WORD AND HE'LL "FIND" THE WRONG END OF MY CANNON.

NO!

NO FIGHTING.

BUT—!

IT'S WHAT WE WERE MADE FOR!

HE CAN HELP US IF HE WANTS.

WE'RE GOING TO FIND JOSEPH.

GUYS. I HATE TO BREAK UP ALL THESE REUNIONS,

BUT THE ENTIRE DOOM SQUAD IS ON ITS WAY DOWN.

FRONTAL ASSAULT! FRONTAL ASSAULT!

NO, WE SHOULD RETREAT. THOSE SHOCK TROOPS WILL DECIMATE US.

CLICK!

THERE'S A SURPRISE.

WHEN DO YOU CHOOSE TO FIGHT, PIPER?

WHEN IT'S WORTH IT!

I SAY WE RUN TO THE SURFACE.

I SAY WE FIGHT OUR WAY UP.

I'M WITH THE FANCY MAN.

SORRY PRETTY LADY.

NO!

WE GO DOWN.

FZZT!

AT LAST.

FZZLT.

TAP TAP

GULP.

REALLY, BOY.

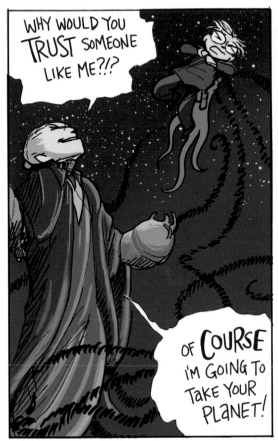

WHY WOULD YOU **TRUST** SOMEONE LIKE ME?!?

OF **COURSE** I'M GOING TO TAKE YOUR PLANET!

YOU DON'T THINK YOUR FRIEND IS GOING TO COME FOR YOU AFTER YOU BETRAYED HER?

WE SCREED AREN'T DIVIDED INTO MALE AND FEMALE, BUT EVEN I CAN SEE YOU HAVE A THING OR TWO TO LEARN ABOUT **WOMEN!**

KICK!

178

friends!

RUUMBLE!

SO YOU GOING TO START FLYING WITH ME AGAIN AFTER THIS?

I HAVE A SHIP.

REMEMBER?

RUUMBLE!

HELP!

I DON'T WANNA SEE THE WORLD!

I WANNA GO HOME!

THE PLANET IS COLLAPSIN', RAGGY!

AIN'T NO HOME TO GO BACK TO!

I MISS MY CELL!

CRACK!

AAAH!

AAH!

NEVER MIND US, SHIPPY! PICK UP THOSE TWO!

192

WHAT ABOUT US?

LOOKS LIKE WE'RE GOING WITH PIPER AFTER ALL.

CRACK!

WE HAVE TO MAKE THE JUMP.

JOSEPH!

PIPER!

IT'S ZITA!

NOW, ROBOT RANDY!

THOOM!

Chapter
Seven

CRRK

SHF.

HEY.

IS—
IS THAT?

"...IS WHEN MY ADVENTURES REALLY BEGAN."

THE ORIGIN AND EVOLUTION OF
ZITA THE SPACEGIRL

Have you ever wondered where characters come from? Some characters seem to spring onto the page, fully formed and ready for adventure. Zita wasn't like that. As a character she took years to develop.

In college I met a REALLY cute girl named Anna. She shared with me some comics that she drew in high school about "Zeta the Spacegirl." They looked like this:

As a way to impress her I began developing the character and I drew comics for her featuring the new Zita the Spacegirl. In the early stories Zita was a time traveler from the future who teamed up with a couple of down-and-out superheroes.

We even had a Zita costume!

And my plan totally worked! That cute girl I made the comics for? She married me.

Later I took those early comics to conventions and showed them to editors, but no one was interested. And so for a time Zita the Spacegirl was forgotten...

Anna in the original Zita the Spacegirl costume

...until I started making webcomics. That's when Zita's personality began taking shape, she started to look younger, and she found her friends Robot Randy and One.

A short Zita story called "If Wishes Were Socks" even appeared in a book called Flight: Explorer.

But one question remained: what was this girl doing traveling through space? What was she after? I realized that this was the story I wanted to tell. And that's the story you've just finished reading.

And what does the future hold for Zita? Only time will tell...

SKETCHES

ACKNOWLEDGMENTS

Special thanks to my mom, who sewed me a leather He-Man baldric and let me wear it to school under my clothes for two years. And to my dad, who helped me build a pair of gliding wings, but made sure I jumped off the retaining wall and not the garage roof. I won the cool parents lottery.

Thanks to my fourth grade teacher, Mrs. Berghoff, for letting me cut out and glue paper antennae to my head instead of paying attention during math class. You could have crushed a young artist there and you didn't.

Thanks to everybody in the little village of Gravagna, where I wrote and drew most of this book. I left my heart there, so please take care of it until I come back.

And thanks, of course, to the crew at First Second! Mark Siegel, Colleen AF Venable, Calista Brill, and Gina Gagliano! You're a pleasure to work with. Thanks also to my indomitable agent, Judy Hansen, for looking after me.

Most of all thanks to Anna and to my girls, Angelica, Zita, Julia, and Ronia. I'd be a smelly old hermit without you guys.

ABOUT THE AUTHOR

Ben Hatke is the father of four daughters and the author of three graphic novels.

He lives in the Shenandoah Valley next to a very old cemetery and he spends an awful lot of time thinking about turtles and robots.

Ben posts stories, art, and comics online at BenHatke.com.